GUM

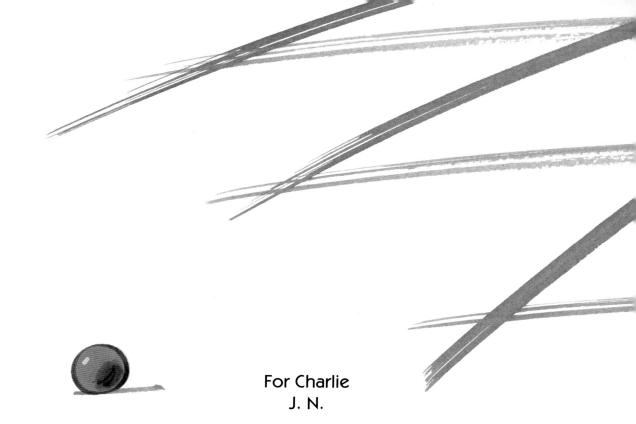

For Charlie
J. N.

First edition 2017

Library of Congress Catalog Card Number pending
ISBN 978-0-7636-7774-9

17 18 19 20 21 22 APS 10 9 8 7 6 5 4 3 2 1

Printed in Humen, Dongguan, China

This book was typeset in Kabel.
The illustrations were done in ink.

Candlewick Press
99 Dover Street
Somerville, Massachusetts 02144

visit us at www.candlewick.com

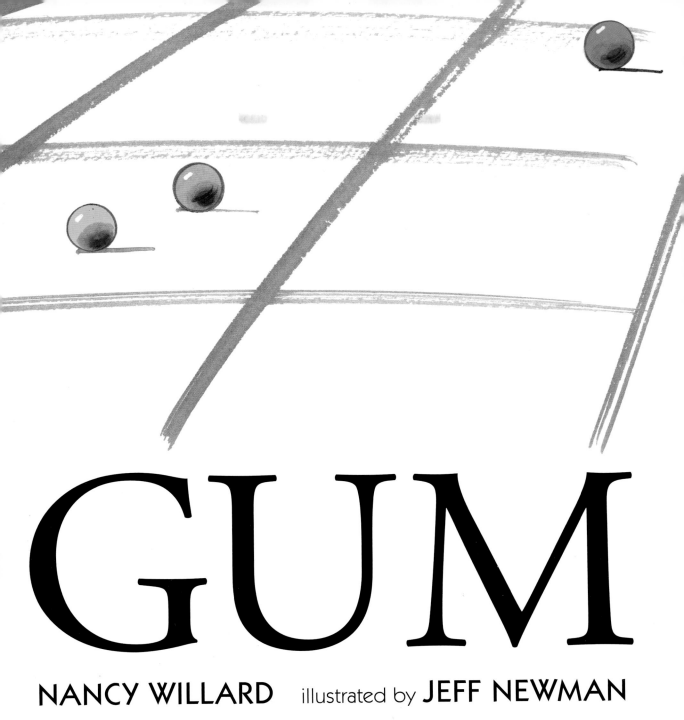

GUM

NANCY WILLARD   illustrated by JEFF NEWMAN

CANDLEWICK PRESS

Here is James, standing by his parents' bed.

"I would like my allowance, please,"
says James.

"What can you do with five quarters
at six in the morning?" asks his mother.

"I can look at them," says James.

His mother counts five quarters into his hand.

"What kind of quarter is this?"
asks James, holding one up.

"Canadian," says his mother.

"Is it lucky?" asks James.

"Oh, yes," says his mother.

James zips his five quarters into
the secret pocket of his pants.

He will need them after school when
he and Danny go to Mr. Wright's store.

Here are James and Danny
in Mr. Wright's store.

When most people put a quarter
in the gumball machine,
they get six gumballs.

Lucky people get six gumballs
and a plastic four-leaf clover.

Very lucky people get six gumballs and a ring.

Very, very lucky people get six gumballs
and a little silver racer.

There is only one silver racer
in Mr. Wright's gumball machine.

Danny and James have kept
their eye on it for a month.

James puts his first quarter
in the slot and
holds out his hand.

Something tumbles
out of the spout.

"Did you get the racer?"
asks Danny.

"Nope," says James.
"Six gumballs. Your turn."

Danny puts his first quarter
in and holds out his hand.

Something clatters
out of the spout.

"Did you get the racer?"
asks James.

"Nope," says Danny.
"I got six gumballs, too.
Your turn."

James puts his second quarter
in and holds out his hand.

Something small and
still slides into it.

"I got something besides gum!"
he says.

He opens his hand.

"You got a ring," says Danny.

James slips the ring on his pinky.

Danny puts his second quarter
in and holds out his hand.

Something round and
raucous runs into it.

"Six gumballs," he says.
"I wish I liked gumballs."

He pockets them anyway,
to use on his marble slider.

James puts his third quarter
in and holds out his hand.

"Did you get the racer?" asks Danny.

James opens his hand.
"No, I got a four-leaf clover."

"It's only got three leaves,"
says Danny. "One broke off."

James pockets the three-leaf clover
without enthusiasm.

Danny puts his third quarter
in and holds out his hand.

The silver racer gleams at the
bottom of the globe. The gumballs
jump and jostle together.

"Did you get the racer?" asks James.

Danny opens his hand.
"No. I got a little wheel."

"But this machine doesn't give
wheels," says James.

"It does *now*," says Danny.

James puts his fourth quarter
in and holds out his hand.

Bing! Bang! Kaboom!

He opens his hand.
"I got more gum,"
he says.
"Your turn."

Danny puts his fourth
and final quarter in
and holds out his hand.

Krish! Crash! Kazoom!

He opens his hand.
"I got gum, too."

James looks at his fifth and last quarter.

"This is a lucky quarter," says James.
"I don't think I want to spend it."

"I bet the next guy will get the racer,"
says Danny.

"This is a Canadian quarter," says James.
"It has a deer on it."

"That racer must be just ready to drop out,"
says Danny. "I bet if you jiggled the machine,
that racer would go plunk on the floor."

James holds his fifth and last quarter
in the slot, just to see if
a Canadian quarter will fit.

In the excitement of seeing that it does,
he loses his grip.

The gumball machine swallows
the Canadian quarter.

Nothing happens.

Nothing comes out at all.

Then out shoot

12 green gumballs,

14 red gumballs,

3 black gumballs,

7 four-leaf clovers,

8 orange gumballs,

10 blue gumballs,

2 erasers,

and 4 rings.

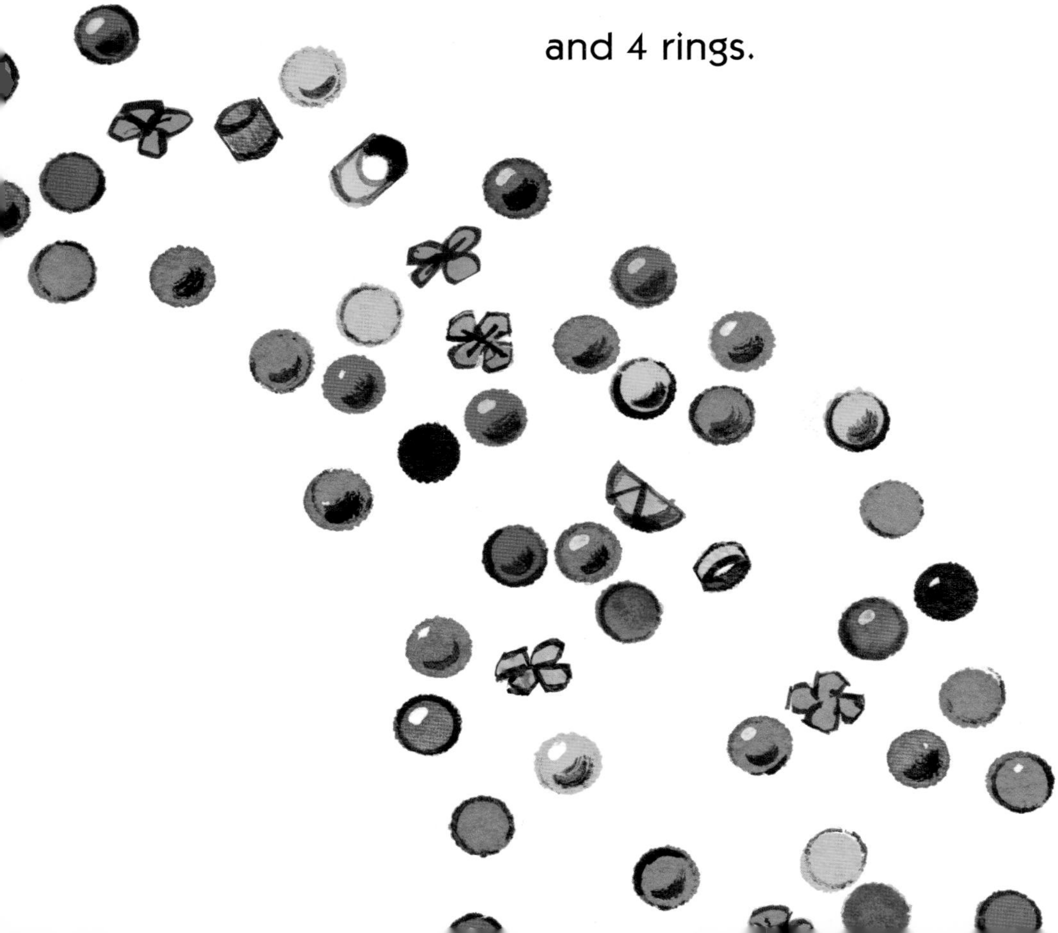

Here is Mr. Wright running.

"What did you do to it?"
he shouts.

"I just put in a quarter,"
says James.

"Grab 'em!" shouts Mr. Wright.

All the customers bend down
and start grabbing.

"Toss 'em in my hat, boys,"
says Mr. Wright.

All the customers throw gumballs
into Mr. Wright's hat.

Here is Mr. Wright's clean floor.

Mr. Wright fetches a sign,
and he hangs it on the gumball machine.

"James never got his gum," says Danny.
"He put a quarter in
but he never got his gum."

"I don't even like gum!" says James.
"I want my quarter back."

Mr. Wright reaches into his pocket
and pulls out a quarter.

James looks at it critically.
"I want the same quarter I put in," he says.
"It's a Canadian quarter. It's lucky."

"How many quarters do you think are in there?"
asks Mr. Wright.
"I can't possibly find your quarter."

James starts to cry.
"I want my quarter back!"

"He wants his quarter back,"
says Danny.

"Now, look," says Mr. Wright,
"if you don't like gum,
you can pick one of the prizes instead."

"OK," says James.
"I'll take the racer."

"What racer?"

"The one at the bottom
of the gumball machine."

Mr. Wright sighs.
He takes a key from his pocket,
unlocks the machine,
and lifts the lid right off.

"It's all yours,"
says Mr. Wright.

James picks up the racer.

"But it's only got three wheels,"
he says.

"Tell you what," says Danny.
"You can borrow my wheel
if I can play with your racer."

"OK," says James. "We'll share it."

"It's a deal," says Danny.

"I knew that quarter was lucky,"
says James.